JACK and the Be...

retold by Stella Williams Nathan

illustrated by Dora Leder

GOLDEN PRESS
Western Publishing Company, Inc.
Racine, Wisconsin

Fifth Printing, 1978

Once upon a time there was a boy who lived with his mother in a tiny cottage. They were very poor. One day his mother said to him, "Jack, you must take our cow to market and sell her so we can buy food."

Jack set out at once. On the way, he met an old man.

"That's a fine-looking cow," said the old man. "If you'll give her to me, I'll give you some magic beans."

Jack stared at the red and yellow beans. How exciting! He took the beans, said good-bye to his cow, and hurried back home.

Jack's mother was very angry when she saw what he had done. "Silly boy!" she exclaimed. "Now we shall starve!" She threw the beans out the window.

When Jack awoke the next morning, his bedroom was dark. He ran to the window and saw a tremendously tall beanstalk outside. It seemed to reach up to the sky.

"They *were* magic beans!" Jack shouted. He jumped out the window and quickly climbed the beanstalk.

At the top, he saw a beautiful castle sparkling in the sun. An old woman greeted him as he hopped off the beanstalk. "Don't go near the castle, young man," she said. "A wicked giant lives there. Long ago, he stole your father's fortune and left him a poor man."

"Then I certainly must get it back!" Jack exclaimed, and he strode right to the castle door.

The giant's wife answered his knock. "If you want food, I'll give you some," she said. "But you must hurry. My husband *eats* boys for breakfast!"

She gave Jack a slice of bread as big as a tabletop. But even as he ate, there began a great noise outside. Jack leaped into a skillet to hide, just as the giant entered, bellowing:

> "Fe, fi, fo, fum,
> I smell the blood of an Englishman.
> Be he alive or be he dead,
> I'll grind his bones to make my bread."

He bent down and peered under the table. "I smell boy!"
"Nonsense," said his wife. "Eat your breakfast."
Grumbling, the giant sat down to ten roasted oxen and
four barrels of milk. Then he shouted, "Wife, bring me my
magic hen!"

His wife hurried to obey.

"Lay, hen, lay!" roared the giant, and the hen laid a golden egg.

"Very good," said the giant, with a mighty yawn. Soon he was sound asleep.

At the first snore, Jack popped out of the skillet, snatched up the hen, and ran off. When he had climbed back down the beanstalk, his mother gasped with wonder.

"Jack!" she exclaimed. "It's your father's magic hen!"

The next day, Jack climbed the beanstalk again. "I'll give you a bite to eat," said the giant's wife when she saw him. "But hurry. The giant is in a terrible temper because he has lost his magic hen."

Jack was eating a tart as big as a fishpond, when the castle began to shake. He leaped into a butter churn, just as the giant entered, bellowing:

"Fe, fi, fo, fum,
I smell the blood of an Englishman.
Be he alive or be he dead,
I'll grind his bones to make my bread."

"Don't tell me you smell boy again," said his wife. "Sit down and eat your breakfast."

Muttering to himself, the giant gobbled twelve roasted pigs and six dozen eggs. Then he shouted, "Wife, bring me my harp!"

Quickly his wife did as she was told.

"Play, harp, play!" commanded the giant, and the harp played such beautiful music that it soon lulled the giant to sleep. At once, Jack jumped out of the butter churn, seized the harp, and ran away.

When he reached the bottom of the beanstalk, his mother was waiting. "Oh, Jack," she said happily, "you have found your father's golden harp!"

When Jack climbed the beanstalk the next morning, the giant's wife was waiting for him. "I'll give you a snack if you wish," she said, "but you are in great danger. The giant lost his harp yesterday, and he's in a terrible rage."

Jack was eating a cupcake as big as a haystack, when he
heard the giant coming. He jumped into a pail and listened
to the terrible roar:

"Fe, fi, fo, fum,
I smell the blood of an Englishman.
Be he alive or be he dead,
I'll grind his bones to make my bread."

"Sit down and eat your breakfast," said the giant's wife. "Then you'll feel better."

Mumbling angrily, the giant ate fifteen roasted ducklings and two hundred sausages.

"Wife," he growled, "fetch my gold. That will cheer me."

For a long time, the giant played with his gold pieces. When at last he closed his eyes, Jack jumped out of the pail, snatched the gold, and ran.

But the giant had been only pretending to sleep. With a roar, he leaped to his feet. "I told you I smelled boy!" he bellowed as he raced after Jack.

Poor Jack ran faster than he had ever run in his life.

"Mother, get the ax ready!" he shouted from the top of the beanstalk.

As he climbed down, the beanstalk began to sway. Jack looked up and saw that the giant was coming down, too. It was such a frightening sight that Jack dropped the gold and tumbled all the way to the ground.

Quick as a wink, he jumped up and took the ax from his mother. Smack! SMACK! The beanstalk snapped in two. There was a great crash, and the giant lay before them—dead!

Jack's mother gave him a hug and told him he was indeed a brave boy. "You have brought back your father's hen, his harp, and his gold," she said. "We shall certainly live happily ever after!"

For who *could* be sad, with a hen to lay golden eggs, a harp to play beautiful music, and gold to buy bread and cheese and—sometimes—strawberry tarts?